Maggie Whitton

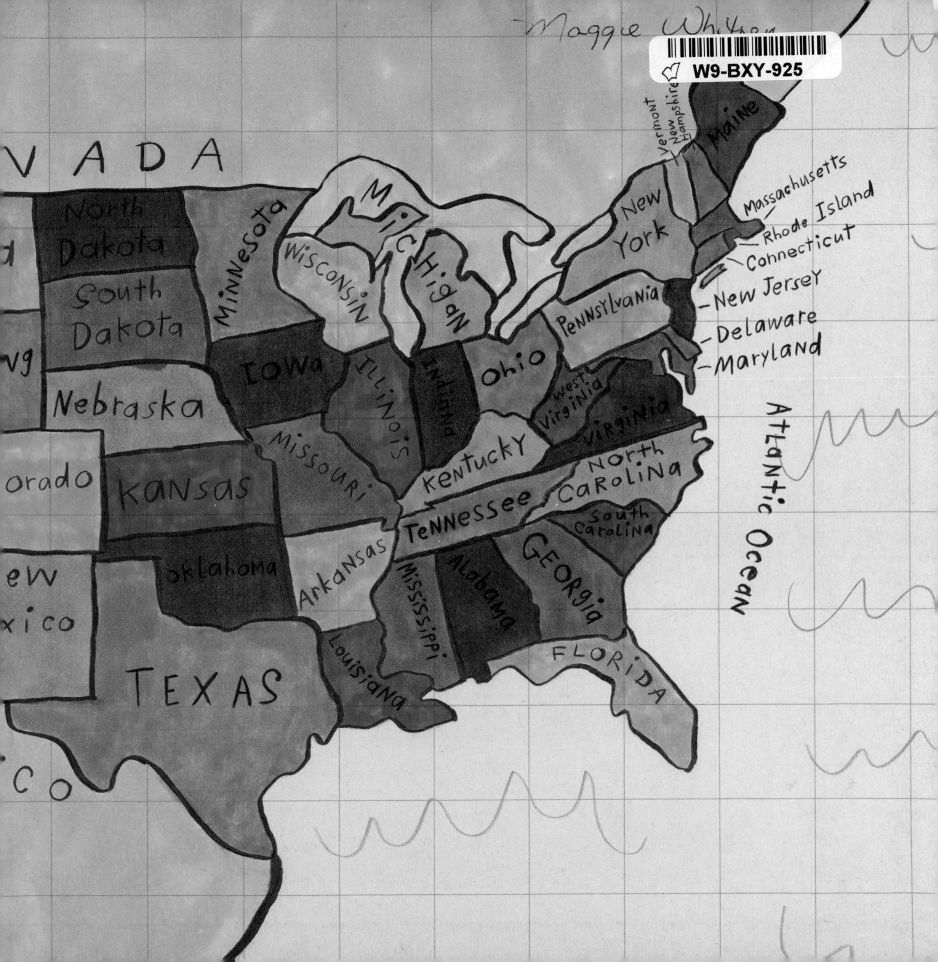

This book is dedicated to my mom.
I love you.
–Laurie

THIS BOOK BELONGS TO:

_____

WHO LIVES IN THE STATE OF:

_____

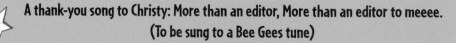

A thank-you song to Christy: More than an editor, More than an editor to meeee.
(To be sung to a Bee Gees tune)

Henry Holt and Company, LLC, *Publishers since 1866*, 115 West 18th Street, New York, New York 10011
Henry Holt is a registered trademark of Henry Holt and Company, LLC

Library of Congress Cataloging-in-Publication Data
Keller, Laurie. The scrambled states of America / Laurie Keller.
Summary: The states become bored with their positions on the map and decide
to change places for a while. Also includes facts about the states.
1. U.S. states—Juvenile fiction. [1. United States—Fiction.] I. Title.
PZ7.K281346Sc 1998 [E]–dc21 97-50418

ISBN 0-8050-5802-8 (hardcover)
10 12 14 16 18 20 19 17 15 13 11
ISBN 0-8050-6831-7 (paperback)
4 6 8 10 12 14 16 18 20 19 17 15 13 11 9 7 5 3

First published in hardcover in 1998 by Henry Holt and Company.
First Owlet paperback edition, 2002

Designed by Meredith Baldwin
Printed in the United States of America on acid-free paper. ∞
The artist used acrylic paint, colored pencils, marker, and collage
on illustration board to create the illustrations for this book.
Factual information about the states on pages 32 to 35 is from
The Doubleday Atlas of the United States of America, by Josephine Bacon (New York: Doubleday, 1990).

the Scrambled States of America

By Laurie Keller

Henry Holt and Company
New York

SUNFLOWER
(State flower of Kansas)

NEBRASKA

KANSAS

Want an acorn?
I love 'em!

"What's wrong?"

his best friend, Nebraska, kindly asked him.
(Nebraska is a very kind state.)

"I don't know," moaned Kansas. "I just feel bored. All day long we just sit here in the middle of the country. We never **GO** anywhere. We never **DO** anything, and we **NEVER** meet any **NEW** states!"

"Hmmmmm . . ." said Nebraska.

"Don't get me wrong,
Nebraska. You're the best
friend a state could have.

But don't you ever want more?
Don't you ever want to see
what else is out there?"

Nebraska's
thought Process

"Yes! Yes, I do!" Nebraska said excitedly.
"And now that you mention it,
I'm sick and tired of hearing
North Dakota and South Dakota
bicker all the time!"

Me, too!

I HAVE A GREAT IDEA!

exclaimed Kansas.

(WOW! His smile is 285 miles wide!)

Kansas
Scale of Miles
0 10 20 30 40 50

"Let's have a party and invite all the other states! You know, one of those get-to-know-you deals. Everyone can bring a favorite dish. We could have music and dancing. . . ."

"That's a GREAT idea!" shrieked Nebraska.
"I wish I'd thought of it myself."

So, with a little help from their neighbors, Missouri and Iowa,
those wacky little midwestern states planned the biggest party ever.

They sent out invitations,

and blew up balloons.

They even hired a band to play.

At last, the big day came, and little by little the states arrived at the party. Nebraska and Kansas were on the welcoming committee, Iowa was in charge of coats, and Missouri and Illinois passed out name tags for each state to wear.

WOW! Those southwestern states can really dance!

CALIFORNIA Fruit Salad

IOWA CORN SURPRISE

IDAHO

Montana

Ohio

New Mexico

Minnesota

TEXAS

Allow me.

Thank you.

Wyoming

Yes! They're divine!

Have you tried the Alabama peanut bars?

This is the third time I've dropped my fork!

Within minutes after their arrival, the states began making friends with each other. They spent hours talking, laughing, dancing, and singing.

It was long into the evening when Idaho and Virginia got up on the stage.

"Excuse me," Idaho said politely. (Idaho is a very polite state.) "Sorry to interrupt, but Virginia and I were just talking and we thought it might be fun if she and I switched places—you know—so we could see a new part of the country."

"Yes," Virginia chimed in. "Then we thought maybe all of you might want to try it, too. What do you think?"

Hello, my name is: COLORADO

Hello, my name is: VIRGINIA

Hello, my name is: NEW M

Hello, my name is: IDAHO

Hello, my name is: FLORIDA

Hello, my name is: CALIFORNIA

A wave of excitement swept through the room.

They could hardly wait.
Immediately, the states made their plans to switch places.
They said their good-byes, and went directly home to pack.

It took the better part of the next morning for the states to move to their new spots, but finally they were settled in. All of the states were much happier now that they were by their new neighbors and in a new part of the country. Oh yes, this was a much better arrangement!

But after a couple of days had passed and all the excitement had died down, the states began to realize that they weren't as happy as they thought.

Florida, who had switched spots with Minnesota, was FREEZING in the frosty northern climate. And Minnesota, who forgot to buy sunscreen, got an awful sunburn.

Alabama, New York, and Indiana—all of whom took California's place—were bothered by an annoying rumbling sound that kept them up all night.

Arizona, who had traded places with South Carolina, was upset because the ocean waves kept ruining her hairdo.

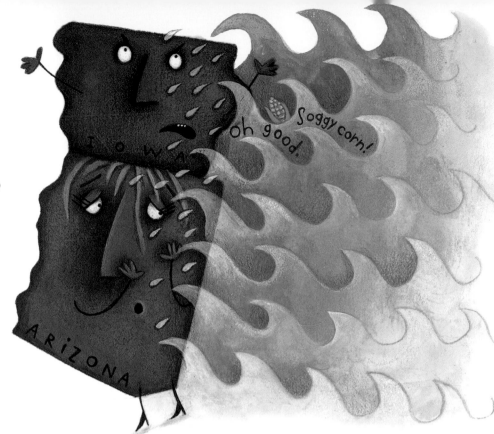

Oh good. Soggy corn!

Her, Potato Head, scratch my back, will ya?

COLORADO

IDAHO

Nevada and Mississippi fell in love so NOTHING bothered them.

Do you want to become MRS.issippi?

I do.

NEVADA

Alaska, who had been wanting a little more interaction with the other states, was irritated by Oklahoma's handle jabbing into his left side and Michigan's thumb tickling his right.

I KNEW this was a bad idea!

Kitchy Kitchy Koo!

MICHIGAN

ALASKA

OKLAHOMA

OKLAHOMA where the wind comes sweepin' down the plain...

OUCH! Watch it!

ARKANSAS

And worst of all, Kansas, who had switched places with Hawaii
because he was sick of being stuck in the middle of the country,
was now stuck in the middle of NOWHERE, feeling lonesome and seasick.

IN THE MIDDLE OF NOWHERE
FEELIN' LONESOME AND SEASICK,

MY GUITAR IS SOGGY
AND I FEEL SO BLUE...

It's
so
sad.

R.I.P.

(And Hawaii was longing for some peace and quiet like in the good old days.)

Well, there was no question in any state's mind about what to do. Everyone wanted to go home! So, even faster than they made the first trip, they packed up their things and hit the road.

Yes, my name is Illinois and I need one airline ticket to...um...well, Illinois... mmmhmmm... no, the "S" is silent.

FLORIDA

Want a ride?

Sure!

Louisiana

ILLINOIS

South Dakota

Do you have any 3's?

GO FISH!

Ohio

BUS STOP

NORTH CAROLINA

As the sun set across the country, all of the states—from A to W— were back in their very own homes. The states were so happy to see their old friends again. They spent the entire evening sharing their new experiences with each other— the good and the bad.

That night, all the states in the country went to bed feeling happy about the new friends they had made but, most of all, feeling very thankful to be home.

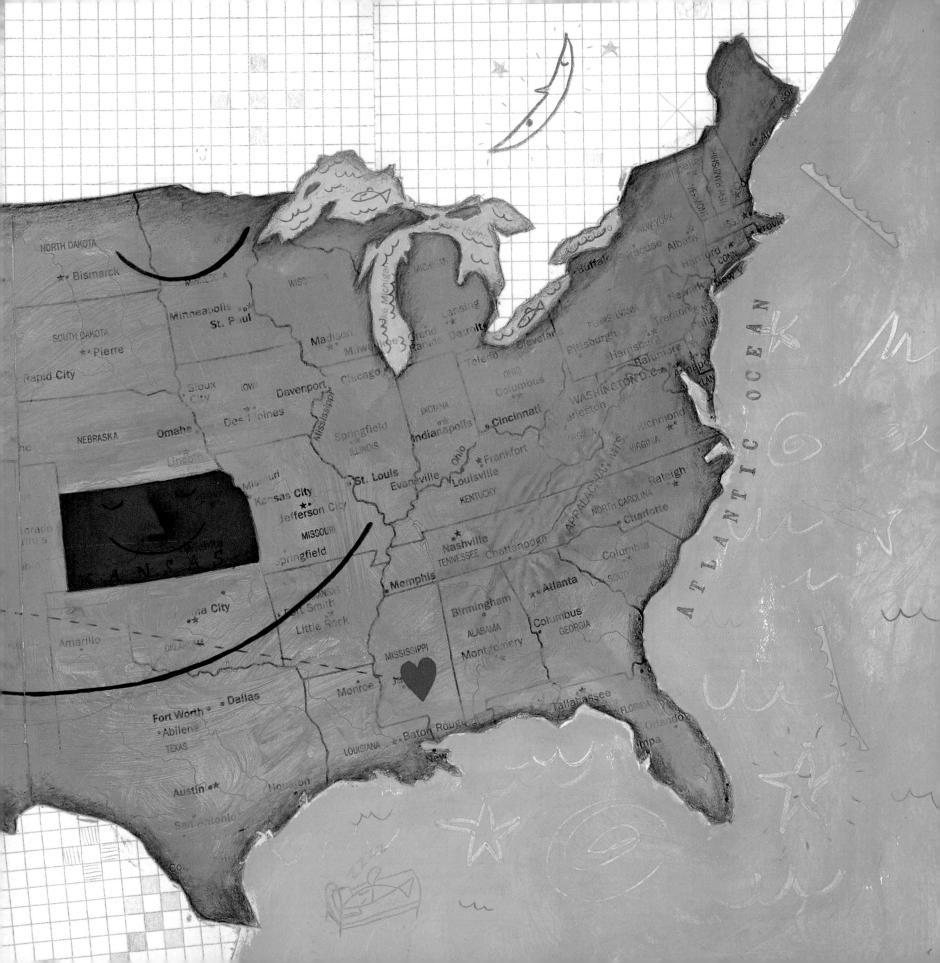